THE MUD PONY

A traditional Skidi Pawnee tale

Retold by Caron Lee Cohen

Illustrated by Shonto Begay

SCHOLASTIC INC., New York

Acknowledgments

THE MUD PONY is one of a number of ancient boy-hero stories told among the Skidi band of the Pawnee Indians of the American Plains. These stories exhibit the Pawnee belief that no matter how lowly one's origin, the path to honor is open through adherence to virtues such as constancy and a humble spirit. This version of *The Mud Pony* was adapted from a longer story in the collection of George A. Dorsey, who recorded the traditions and tales of the Skidi Pawnee between 1899 and 1902. It was told to him by Yellow-Calf.

The author gratefully acknowledges the research assistance of the Nebraska State Historical Society, the Museum of Science in Boston, the American Museum of Natural History, and innumerable branches and services of The New York Public Library in the preparation of this book. Special thanks to Dr. James Smith at the Museum of the American Indian in New York City for his invaluable help.

Text copyright © 1988 by Caron Lee Cohen.
Illustrations copyright © 1988 by Shonto Begay.
Design by Theresa Fitzgerald.
All rights reserved. Published by Scholastic Inc.
SCHOLASTIC HARDCOVER is a registered trademark of Scholastic Inc.

Library of Congress Cataloging-in-Publication Data
Cohen, Caron Lee.
The mud pony.

Summary: A poor boy becomes a powerful leader when Mother Earth
turns his mud pony into a real one,
but after the pony turns back to mud,
he must find his own strength.
1. Pawnee Indians—Legends.   2. Indians of North America—Great Plains—Legends.
[1. Pawnee Indians—Legends.   2. Indians of North America—Legends.   3. Ponies—Folklore]
I. Begay, Shonto, ill.   II. Title.
E99.P3C64 1988   398.2'08997 [E]   87-23451
ISBN 0-590-41525-5

12 11 10 9 8 7 6 5 4 3 2 1   8 9/8 0 1 2 3/9

Printed in Japan   10
First Scholastic printing, September 1988

For my husband Bill with love
—C.L.C.

In memory of my brother, Wilson,
and my sister, Dorothy.
—S.B.

THERE WAS ONCE a poor boy in an Indian camp who would watch by the creek as other boys watered their ponies. More than anything, he longed for a pony of his own.

So at last the boy crossed the creek, dug the wet earth, and shaped a pony out of mud. He gave it a white clay face. He loved his mud pony. Every day he went to it and took care of it as if it were real.

One day while the boy was with his mud pony, scouts rode into camp. "We've sighted buffalo several days' journey west," they said. The people broke camp, for they would starve in the months ahead if they didn't hunt the buffalo. The boy's parents looked everywhere, but they couldn't find him. Finally, they had to leave without him.

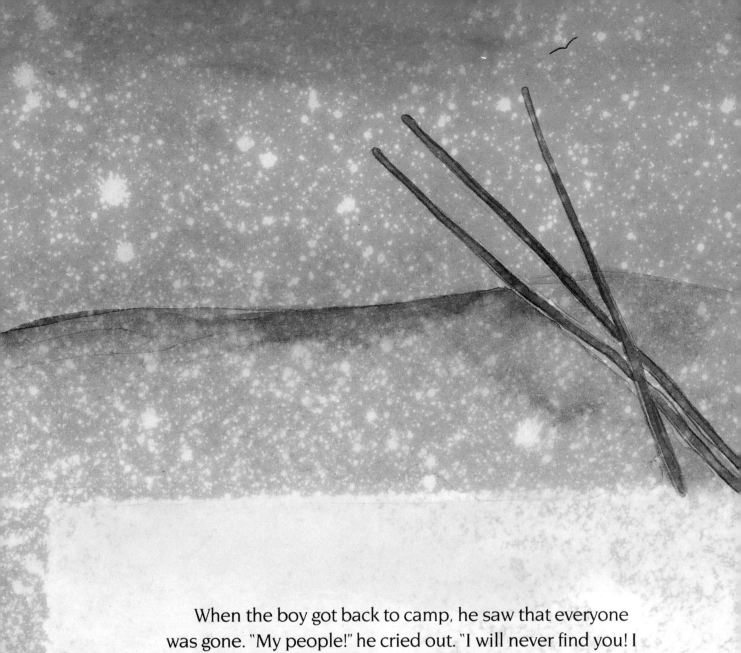

When the boy got back to camp, he saw that everyone was gone. "My people!" he cried out. "I will never find you! I am all alone!" He wandered, heartsick and hungry, around the empty camp, picking up scraps of dried meat and a tattered old blanket someone had thrown away. He ate, then huddled up in the blanket and cried himself to sleep.

As he slept, he dreamt his mud pony was alive and spoke to him: "My son, you are not alone. Mother Earth has given me to you. I am part of her."

When the boy woke at daybreak in the empty camp, he cried for his people. Then he went to his mud pony and could hardly believe his eyes! The white-faced pony was alive, tossing her mane and pawing the ground.

She spoke like the pony in his dream: "My son, you are not alone. Mother Earth has given me to you. I am part of her. You must do as I say, and someday you will be a chief among your people. They are far away. Get on my back, and I will take you to them. But do not try to guide me, for I know where to go."

For three days they journeyed over the plains. The boy was worn and hungry, but he would not give up; he let the pony guide him.

Then at the third nightfall, the boy saw smoke curling up from tepees in a camp. They had reached his people.

"Go and find your parents," said the pony. "But leave them before dawn; it is not time yet for the others to see you. I will be waiting in the hills. Now cover me with the blanket to protect me from the rain, for I am part of Mother Earth."

The boy went into the camp. He wandered among the tepees until he found the smallest one. He went in and threw dried grass into the fire, so a blaze went up. In the fire's light he saw his mother and woke her.

"Here I am," he said.

She touched him and tears came into her eyes. Then his father woke and marveled at how the boy had found them when they had gone so far away.

Before dawn the boy told his parents, "I must go now. On my own." He left them, but from the hills he turned and watched as the people broke camp to continue on their way to the buffalo. At last they disappeared.

For three more days the boy and the pony journeyed over the plains. The boy was weary and had no food at all, but he kept on going.

Finally at the third nightfall, he saw a camp in the distance. "There are your people," the pony said. "It is time that you join them. Ride me into the camp."

The boy did. And all the people came out of their tepees, astonished to see him.

A war chief invited him into a big tepee. There was soup and dried meat and two buffalo horn spoons in a wooden bowl. They ate together.

"*Nawa, tiki!*" the war chief saluted him. "You
journeyed over strange land, starving and alone, and yet
you found us! You have a gift, a great power. And now you
must help our people. An enemy has attacked us on our
way west, killing men, keeping us from reaching the buffalo.
At daybreak you must join us in battle."

When the boy left the big tepee, he trembled. But the pony spoke to him: "My son, do not be afraid. For I am part of Mother Earth. And the enemy's arrows can never pierce the earth. Put earth all over your body, and you will not be hurt."

At daybreak he covered his body with earth and rode the pony straight into the fight. There was a fierce battle, but he led his people to victory. At last the people were free for the hunt, and the boy on the white-faced pony showed the way, capturing more buffalo than any of the grown men.

Years passed, and always the boy let his pony guide
him. Always he was a powerful leader. Finally, he was made
a chief! As a chief, he had a corral full of fine horses, but the
white-faced pony was his great gift. He tied many eagle
feathers into her mane and tail. And every nightfall he care-
fully covered her with a blanket to protect her from rain.

Then one night while he slept the pony came to him in a dream: "My son, now you are a chief among your people, a chief with the power of Mother Earth. It is Mother Earth who gives you the power, and not I. I am part of her, and it is time that I go back to her. You must let me go."

The chief got up in the dark and went to his pony. She pawed the ground and tossed her mane in the wind.
"Take my blanket," she said. He did. Then he went to his tepee.

Just before daybreak, he woke to shrill winds and
rushing rain. He ran to his corral, and looked everywhere
for his white-faced pony. He couldn't find her.

Then as the morning light broke over the wet earth,
the chief saw a patch of white clay. And through the wind,
he heard a voice:

"I am here, your Mother Earth. You are not alone!"